A Beginning-to-Read Book

It's St. Patrick's Day, Dear Dragon

by Margaret Hillert

Illustrated by David Schimmell

NORWOOD HOUSE PRESS

DEAR CAREGIVER, The *Beginning-to-Read* series is a carefully written collection of readers, many of which you may remember from your own childhood. This book, *It's St. Patrick's Day, Dear Dragon*, was written over 30 years after the first *Dear Dragon* books were published. The *New Dear Dragon* series features the same elements of the earlier books, such as text comprised of common sight words. These sight words provide your child with ample practice reading the words that appear most frequently in written text. The many additional details in the pictures enhance the story and offer the opportunity for you to help your child expand oral language skills and develop comprehension.

Begin by reading the story to your child, followed by letting him or her read familiar words and soon your child will be able to read the story independently. At each step of the way, be sure to praise your reader's efforts to build his or her confidence as an independent reader. Discuss the pictures and encourage your child to make connections between the story and his or her own life. At the end of the story, you will find reading activities and a word list that will help your child practice and strengthen beginning reading skills.

Above all, the most important part of the reading experience is to have fun and enjoy it!

Shannon Cannon

Shannon Cannon,
Literacy Consultant

Norwood House Press • P.O. Box 316598 • Chicago, Illinois 60631
For more information about Norwood House Press please visit our website at *www.norwoodhousepress.com* or call 866-565-2900.

Designer: The Design Lab

LIBRARY OF CONGRESS CATALOGING-IN-PUBLICATION DATA
   Hillert, Margaret.
    It's St. Patrick's Day, dear dragon / Margaret Hillert ; illustrated by David Schimmell.
     p. cm. — (A beginning-to-read book)
    Summary: "A boy and his pet dragon celebrate St. Patrick's Day by finding things that are green"—Provided by publisher.
    ISBN-13: 978-1-59953-161-8 (library edition : alk. paper)
    ISBN-10: 1-59953-161-5 (library edition : alk. paper)
   [1. Dragons—Fiction. 2. Saint Patrick's Day--Fiction. 3. Green—Fiction.] I. Schimmell, David, ill. II. Title. III. Title: It is Saint Patrick's Day, dear dragon.
   PZ7.H558Its 2008
   [E]—dc22   2007037022
Manufactured in the United States of America in North Mankato, Minnesota.
295R—062016

Green, green, green.
I like green.
You are green.
I like you.

3

Look down here.
Here is something green.
Little and green.

It is little now.
But it will get big.
Big and pretty.

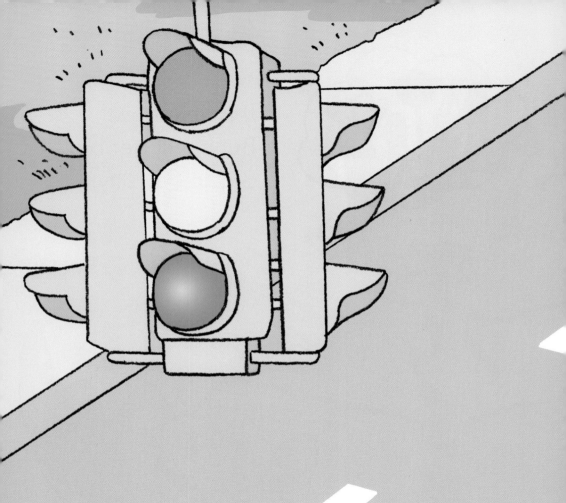

And look up here.
Look up, up, up.
That is green, too.

It can help us.
We can go now.
We can walk now.

7

We can go in here.
We can play here.
We can have fun in here.

I have something to play with.
You will like it.
It can go up.

Oh, oh, oh.
Look at this.
This is funny.
It looks like you.

Up, up, up.
See it go.
We will have to run, run, run.

Here. I will put this on you.
Now run, run, run.
You can do it, too.

Oh, no.
Look at it now.
It will go away, away, away.
We can not get it.

But we can get
something for Mother.
Something pretty.

Look at this.
It is pretty and green.
Mother will like this.

Mother, Mother.
Where are you?
Look what we have
for you.

20

Oh, how pretty.
I like it.
I like it.
I like it.

I have something for you, too.
Something good to eat.

One for me.
One for you,
And that one looks like you.

Here comes Father.
Father, Father,
do you have
something green?

24

Oh, you do.
You do.
It is pretty.

Yes, it is pretty.
And here are two for you.
See this and this.

Here you are with me.
And here I am with you.
Oh, what a lucky St. Patrick's Day,
dear dragon.

READING REINFORCEMENT

The following activities support the findings of the National Reading Panel that determined the most effective components for reading instruction are: Phonemic Awareness, Phonics, Vocabulary, Fluency, and Text Comprehension.

Phonemic Awareness: The long /ē/ sound

Sound Substitution: Say the words on the left to your child. Ask your child to repeat the word, changing the short /ĕ/ sound to a long /ē/ sound:

pet = Pete	bed = bead	lest = least	check = cheek
fed = feed	ten = teen	fell = feel	best = beast
led = lead	stem = steam	met = meet/meat	sell = seal
net = neat	set = seat	tell = teal	

Phonics: The long /ē/ spelling

1. Make three columns on a blank sheet of paper and label each with these spellings for long /ē/: e, ee, ea

2. Write the following words on separate index cards:

be	green	tree	bean	eat
me	jeep	meat	dear	tea
seed	queen	we	treat	leaf
meet	cheese	sleep	peach	each
lean	see	sea	weak	

3. Ask your child to read each word and place the card under the column heading that represents the long /ē/ spelling in the word.

Vocabulary: Sense Words

1. Write each of the following words on index cards and read them aloud to your child. Ask your child to repeat the words after you: see, hear, feel, smell, taste.

2. Point to each word and ask your child to describe something she/he does to use that sense.

3. Read the following questions and statements aloud and ask your child to point to the word that describes the corresponding sense.

When the boy looked at the green leaves, what sense did he use? (see)

Which senses did they use when the wind blew the kite in the air? (hear, feel, see)

Which senses did they use when they bought shamrocks at the flower shop? (see, smell)

When father gave the boy and the dragon green pins, what senses did they use? (see, feel)

Which senses did they use when mother gave them the cupcakes? (see, smell, feel, taste)

Fluency: Choral Reading

1. Reread the story with your child at least two more times while your child tracks the print by running a finger under the words as they are read. Ask your child to read the words he or she knows with you.

2. Reread the story aloud together. Be careful to read at a rate that your child can keep up with.

3. Repeat choral reading. Allow your child to be the lead reader, and ask him or her to change from a whisper to a loud voice while you follow along and change your voice.

Text Comprehension: Discussion Time

1. Ask your child to retell the sequence of events in the story.

2. To check comprehension, ask your child the following questions:
   - Why were there so many green things in this story?
   - What kind of day does it need to be to fly a kite?
   - How do you think mother felt when they gave her the potted plant? How do you know?
   - Have you ever celebrated St. Patrick's Day? What did you do?

WORD LIST

It's St. Patrick's Day, Dear Dragon uses the **67** words listed below.
This list can be used to practice reading the words that appear in the text.
You may wish to write the words on index cards and use them to help your
child build automatic word recognition. Regular practice with these words
will enhance your child's fluency in reading connected text.

a	eat	I	oh	that
am		in	on	this
and	Father	is	one	to
are	for	it		too
at	fun		Patrick's	two
away	funny	like	play	
		little	pretty	up
big	get	look(s)	put	us
but	go	lucky		
	good		run	walk
can	green	me		we
comes		Mother	St.	what
	have		see	where
day	help	no	something	will
dear	here	not		with
down	how	now		
do				yes
dragon				you

ABOUT THE AUTHOR Margaret Hillert has written over 80 books for
children who are just learning to read. Her books
have been translated into many different languages and over a million children
throughout the world have read her books. She first started writing poetry as
a child and has continued to write for children and adults throughout her life. A
first grade teacher for 34 years, Margaret is now retired from teaching and lives in
Michigan where she likes to write, take walks in the morning, and care for her three cats.

Photograph by Glenna Washburn

ABOUT THE ADVISER Shannon Cannon contributed the activities pages that appear in
this book. Shannon serves as a literacy consultant and provides
staff development to help improve reading instruction. She is a frequent presenter at educational
conferences and workshops. Prior to this she worked as an elementary school teacher and as
president of a curriculum publishing company.